D E F

K L M

ACROSS THE

BIG COUNTRY

An Alphabet Adventure with DONALD DUCK

by G. Harrison Olesen

Random House 🏠 New York

Copyright © 1972 by Walt Disney Productions • All rights reserved under International and Pan-American Copyright Conventions. Published in the United States by Random House, Inc., New York, and simultaneously in Canada by Random House of Canada Limited, Toronto.

Library of Congress Cataloging in Publication Data

Olesen, G. Harrison   Across the big country.

Donald Duck's airplane trip across the country provides situations which stress each letter of the alphabet.

[1. Alphabet books] PZ7.A1858 [E] 72-4930
ISBN 0-394-82519-5   ISBN 0-394-92519-x (lib. bdg.)

Manufactured in the United States of America

T U V
0 1 2 3 4 5 6 7 8 9

Aa

An airport.
An airplane.
Donald Duck's airplane.
Donald Duck's airplane is in the air.
Donald is going away,
away on his trip across the big country.
All his friends wave good-by to Donald.

Bb

Donald sees a balloon—
a big, beautiful balloon.
He sees a big, beautiful bear
in the big, beautiful balloon.
He also sees a bunny . . .
a funny bunny.
And a beaver.
The bear is boss of the balloon.
He is busy.

BYE BYE BIG BIRD!

The bunny and beaver have little balloons.

Donald flies by carefully.

He must not burst the big balloon.

Cc

"There is a circus!" Donald calls.
A boy on a cow—a cowboy.
A clown with a carrot is on the camel.
Look, a car!
A car with clowns,
a car with clown cops.

CRASH!

Dd

There is a dog.
A dirty dog. A dreadfully dirty dog.
He has a doll. A dirty doll.
A dreadfully dirty doll.

Drum, Duck, drum!
Dance, Duck, dance!

E e

Early every evening,
Ellie Elephant enjoys
a trip down the east hill.
What an elegant elephant!
She has three poles . . .
eight shiny buttons . . .
and even large earmuffs.

EH ?

EGAD!

Eight o'clock.
Time to eat.
Look! An egg.
A great big egg.
An eagle's egg.

Oh, oh! Mother Eagle!
Excuse me!

F f

Fish.
Flying fish. Four flying fish.

A frog. A frying pan. A flag.
A flag-waving,
fish-frying *frog!*

G g

Good! Goofy's gasoline station.
Donald Duck needs gas.
Go ahead, Goofy! Get the gas going!

A green goose pours
the first can of gas.
A gray goose is on the way, too.
The third goose will fly up next.
Donald will get his gas
without going near the ground.

High over the hill
Donald sees a hippo.
He sees a heap of hippos.
It's a "hippo holiday!"
One hippo has a horn.
Another hippo has a harp.
A third hippo
has a harmonica,
a huge harmonica.
Hey! A hippo
with a hamburger.

The happy hippos hop and hum as Donald hurries away.

Ice! A lake of ice.

"I love to ice skate," Donald says.

Look at Irving Insect!

What a good ice skater he is!

Other ice skaters are buying ice cream

at Ivan's Ice Cream Igloo.

J j

BIG JOKE!

A jumping contest.
Jerry Rhino jumps over a lot of jugs.
Jump, Jerry!
Jiminy Cricket juggles jars of jam and jelly.
Give Jerry the jelly, Jiminy!

K k

Look out, Donald. A kite.
Lots of kites. . . .
A green kite. A blue kite. A red kite.
Who is flying the kites?
The king is flying kites
from his kitchen.
A fine kettle of kites.

A kangaroo in a kangaroo flies a kite.
Two kittens, in the kangaroo's kite,
fly two kites.

Look!
A very large lion.
A little lamb.
The lion licks his lips.

Lions love lamb lollipops.
Poor little lamb!

The lion leaps. The lamb runs.
Donald leans over. He lassos the lion.
Lucky little lamb!

Mm

Donald flies many more miles.
Right into the middle
of many monkey mailmen.
Donald must help the monkeys.
He must fly the mail.
"Monkeys," said Donald,
"bring me the mail."

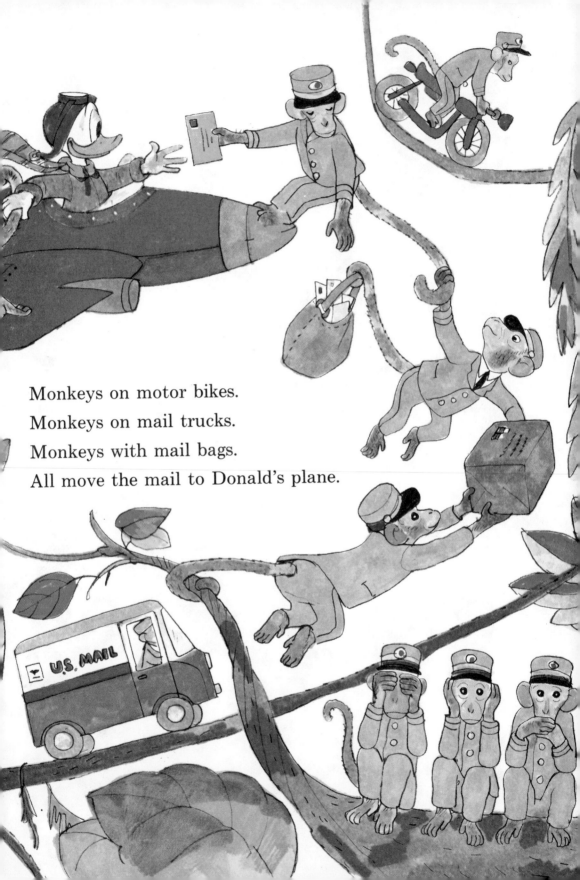

Monkeys on motor bikes.
Monkeys on mail trucks.
Monkeys with mail bags.
All move the mail to Donald's plane.

N n

Now Donald sees something new.
What is it?
Is it a nose?
It is a nose!
A big nose!
A nose that big is news.
It is an elephant's nose.
Nine nice birds read the news
on the elephant's nose.

O o

There is an ox.

He is wearing overalls.

The ox has an ax.

The ox swings the ax!

here is an oak tree.

scar Owl lives in the oak tree.

h, oh! There goes the old oak tree.

ood-by, old oak tree!

Donald and his plane pass a party.
A picnic party.
Pelican eats pies . . .
pecan pies, pumpkin pies, peach pies.
Panda eats pancakes—
piles and piles of pancakes.

Pig eats pizza.

Penguin eats pretty peas in pods.

Please pass a plate of pears to the pilot.

Polly wants popcorn.

Qq

The quilt-covered queen wakes up.
Donald is flying past her window.
"Quiet!" she roars. "Quit flying here!"

Rr

In the rain
Donald sees a rooster.
A real rooster
on a red rooster.
A rooster on a rooster
resting on the roof.

S

Donald soars into the sky.

He sees seven skywriters.

Seven skunk skywriters.

Seven skunk skywriters in silly sweaters.

SKUNKS SMELL SWEET

T t

Donald is on TV.

Ten tame tigers watch Donald flying on TV.

"Three cheers for Donald!" they cry.

"Thank you," says Donald.

U u

There is an umbrella.
Under the umbrella is an umpire.
Ulysses Umpire.
What an unusual game!
The catcher is upside down.

The umpire's uncle is the batter.
He uses a ukulele for a bat.
The third baseman wears underwear.
"Unreal, unbelievable," Donald says,
as he flies away.

V v

Donald is very close to home.
He hears music
coming from the valley.
Victor Vulture in a vest
is playing the violin.
Violet Vulture is playing the viola.
"Very good music!" says Donald.

WOW!

W w

A wet, white bird watches a walrus.
A walrus with a whistle on a whale.

X x

Xmas. Donald is home.
Presents for everybody.
A xylophone.
An x-ray machine.

MERRY XMAS

Y y

Yellow Yo-Yos.
And a yak.
Yes, a young, yawning yak.

Z z

And a zany zebra,
adding up zeros.
Zowie!